Polar Star

Sally Grindley

Illustrated by John Butler

ORCHARD BOOKS

Deep beneath the frozen Arctic
snow, Polar Star stirred in the cosy
den she had built to protect herself
from the winter cold.

Her fur was thicker than it had
ever been and she was fat, ready
to feed her cubs when they were
born. She would not eat again
until the spring.

Polar Star gave birth to Snowball and Snowflake. They were small as kittens, blind and helpless. They nuzzled their way through their mother's fur until they reached her milk and fed hungrily, then they slept.

For four months Polar Star fed and nursed her cubs and soon they grew as big as puppies.

Up above, the days were growing lighter and the winds were less harsh. The time had come to leave the den.

Polar Star broke through the walls and gazed at the sparkling white world before her. She hauled herself out into the freezing air and threw herself into the snow, rolling over and over, a joyful jumble of fur and legs.

Snowball and Snowflake watched spellbound from the den, blinking furiously in the bright sunlight and squealing.

They watched and waited, then they stumbled outside, step by slippery step, following their mother.

As the days passed, they
quickly became bundles of
trouble as they clambered
on top of Polar Star and
wrestled with each other.
Their favourite game was
to climb a steep slope and
toboggan down, slipping
and sliding on their tummies.

But now it was time for Polar Star to find food for herself. She set out, venturing over land and onto the treacherous sea ice. She wove her way across the frozen wilderness, keeping her cubs close by and stopping only to feed them and to sleep.

Soon they were far from land. Polar Star left her cubs to play and ambled to the edge of the ice. Snowball and Snowflake watched as their mother gave a great shudder of joy and plunged beneath the waves.

Moments later she heaved herself out, shook herself dry, and sniffed her way across the ice in search of food.

At last she stopped by a large hole, sat and waited. Her wait was rewarded when the head of a seal popped up through the hole. She acted quickly. One cuff of her giant paw sent the seal crashing against the ice, and Polar Star had her first meal in five months.

While Snowball watched his mother, Snowflake
wandered over to the water's edge, unaware that
danger was closing in fast. A huge male Polar bear
was striding towards her. He was hungry and would
think nothing of snatching a cub for food.

Snowball saw the big male bear and ran, squealing, to his mother. Polar Star turned in alarm. She saw the male bear and rose up on her hind legs, growling a terrible growl.

The male bear hesitated for a second, then grabbed at Snowflake. Polar Star charged, but the male bear reared up on to his hind legs and struck her and struck her again. Polar Star fell backwards. Then she hurled herself at the male bear, pummelling him with her paws and screaming with fury.

At last the male bear backed away, shaken by her fearlessness, and began to lick his wounds.

Polar Star didn't waste any time, she gathered the terrified cubs to her and raced them away across the ice.

They walked for miles. At last darkness swept round them
and Polar Star scoured the landscape for somewhere to shelter.

She tunnelled into a mound of drifted snow and built a den. There, Snowball and Snowflake snuggled up tight in the folds of her enormous body and felt safe again.

The world outside was an exciting place, but it was full of danger. Polar Star would be there to protect her cubs until they were old enough and wise enough to look after themselves.

Polar Bear Facts

Polar bears survive in the freezing cold of the high Arctic, spending
most of their time on pack ice far from land. Their thick white fur
covers a layer of fat that keeps them warm. They are excellent
swimmers and can spend hours in the icy waters.

They are the largest meat-eating land mammals. Polar bears feed mostly
on seals, grabbing them when they come up for air at breathing holes
in the ice. They may even kill small whales and walruses.

In November and December, pregnant female bears dig dens
in the snow and disappear inside until the following March or April.
During that time, they give birth to one, two, or sometimes
three tiny cubs. The cubs feed on their mother's milk.
When they are about three months old, the cubs leave the den with
their mother. They stay with her until they are just over two years old.

The Polar bear cubs' greatest enemies are hungry male Polar
bears, for whom they are an easy source of food.
The only enemy adult Polar bears have is man.